DAD SCHOOL

To my dad, Mel Harless, who graduated with highest honors from Dad School.
—R.V.S.

For my Craig and the wise and wonderful dads in our life,
Ruben Garcia and Omer Burris.
—P.B.

Text copyright © 2016 by Rebecca Van Slyke
Cover art and interior illustrations copyright © 2016 by Priscilla Burris

All rights reserved. Published in the United States by Dragonfly Books, an imprint of Random House Children's Books, a division of
Penguin Random House LLC, New York. Originally published in hardcover in the United States by Doubleday, an imprint of
Random House Children's Books, a division of Penguin Random House LLC, New York, in 2016.

Dragonfly Books and colophon are registered trademarks of Penguin Random House LLC.

Visit us on the Web! rhcbooks.com

Educators and librarians, for a variety of teaching tools, visit us at RHTeachersLibrarians.com

Library of Congress Cataloging-in-Publication Data
Van Slyke, Rebecca.
Dad School / by Rebecca Van Slyke ; illustrated by Priscilla Burris. — First edition.
pages cm
Summary: A child imagines what lessons are taught at Dad School, from learning how to give piggybacks to singing along to the radio.
ISBN 978-0-385-38895-5 (hc) — ISBN 978-0-385-38896-2 (glb) — ISBN 978-0-385-38897-9 (ebk)
[1. Fathers—Fiction. 2. Schools—Fiction.] I. Burris, Priscilla, illustrator. II. Title.
PZ7.1.V39Dad 2016 [E]—dc23 2015001491

ISBN 978-0-593-37439-9 (pbk.)

MANUFACTURED IN CHINA
10 9 8 7 6 5 4 3 2 1
First Dragonfly Books Edition

DAD SCHOOL

Rebecca Van Slyke

Illustrated by

Priscilla Burris

MY Dad

Dragonfly Books ⸻ New York

W hen I go to school,
I learn how to write my name,
paint pictures,

and play games.

My dad says he went to school, too.

Dad

I think he went to
Dad School.

At Dad School, I think they learn how to fix boo-boos,

how to mend leaky faucets,

and how to make huge snacks, like double-decker ham-and-cheese sandwiches with pickles and potato chips.

At Dad School, they also learn how to sing along with old songs on the radio

and how to teach me
to ride a two-wheeler.

Dads should never be late to Dad School, because they might miss how to make really big muscles,

or how to throw their kids
up in the air and catch them.

At Dad School, they learn how to do more than one thing at a time,
like making breakfast and checking my homework,

and playing Go Fish while paying the bills.

Sometimes I think my
dad missed the days
they taught about
matching clothes,
brushing hair,
and cleaning the
bathroom.

But I'm glad he was there when they taught about making ice cream sundaes,

telling silly stories,

and giving
piggyback rides
when I'm too
tired to walk
anymore.

My dad must have been the best student at Dad School.

My dad has another job, too.

But he says
his **favorite** job,

his **best** job,

his **most important** job

is the job he learned at
Dad School:

being my dad.